The Waterhole

Archie's House

The Plane

The Homestead

Mitzi's

Ned's Caravan

The Windmill

Published by Ladybird Books Ltd
A Penguin Company
80 Strand, London WC2R 0RL
Penguin Books Australia Ltd., Camberwell, Victoria, Australia
Penguin Group (NZ) cnr Airborne and Rosedale Roads,
Albany, Auckland 1310, New Zealand.

www.ladybird.co.uk

3 5 7 9 10 8 6 4 2

What Mitzi Wants

Ladybird

One day in the outback, Mitzi had gone to buy some groceries for the Koala Brothers.

She was about to walk into Sammy's shop, when she suddenly spotted the most amazing thing in the window! It was a beautiful toy carousel, spinning around. Mitzi had never seen anything so wonderful in her life!

Mitzi went straight inside to see
Sammy. "That carousel in the
window," she said. "I'll take it!"
and she slapped some silver coins
down on the counter.

"Umm . . . I'm afraid that's not
enough, Mitzi," said Sammy. "It's
fifteen coins for the carousel."

Mitzi stepped back in surprise. "Can't I have it anyway? I really want it!"

Sammy shook his head. "Maybe if you saved up enough pocket money you could afford to buy it," he suggested.

"But I want it NOW!" said Mitzi. "It's not fair!" And with that, she walked out.

Back at the Homestead Mitzi shook
out every last coin from her piggy
bank, but she *still* didn't have
enough to buy the carousel.

"Hi Mitzi," called Frank. "Did you
get the tea and bread?"

"Did you get the chocolate for my
cake?" Buster added.

Mitzi admitted that she hadn't. "But
I saw the most amazing carousel in
Sammy's shop today, and I'm going
to buy it!" she told them. But no
matter how many times she counted,
she still didn't have fifteen coins in
her money box.

Frank thought for a moment.
"You know, Mitzi, you could earn some extra pocket money by doing little jobs for friends."

"Like what?" sighed Mitzi. "I can't mend cars or build houses."

"Not those kinds of jobs, Mitzi,"
said Buster. "Little jobs, like . . .
like cleaning Ned's windows!"

"That's a good idea!" Mitzi agreed.
"But who else could I help?"

"Leave it to us!" said the
Koala Brothers.

Bright and early the next morning, Frank and Buster took off for town in their yellow plane.

Their first stop was Sammy's shop, since Mitzi had forgotten to get the chocolate Buster needed for his cake! But although Buster searched Sammy's shelves from top to bottom, he couldn't find the chocolate anywhere.

"Sorry, Buster," sighed Sammy. "It's Josie's day off and things have got in a bit of a mess."

"Maybe you need some help," Frank suggested. "What about Mitzi?"

"Great idea!" cried Sammy. "Send her over right away!"

Outside Sammy's shop, the Koala
Brothers saw George leaving the
post office. He was trying to carry
an enormous pile of parcels.

"That's quite a load, George," said
Frank.

"Yes, indeedy," puffed George. "I
could do with a little help today!"

Frank smiled at his brother. "We know just the person!"

Around the corner, the Koala Brothers came across their friend Alice, all covered in oil. "I've just fixed my scooter," she explained. "Now it needs a good clean, but I'm *so* tired!"

"Mitzi'll do it for you!" beamed Buster.

Back at the homestead, Mitzi was washing Ned's windows so well he thought she might wear out the glass! Then Frank and Buster came back with big smiles on their faces.

"Sammy, George and Alice all have jobs for you to do," said Buster.

Frank grinned. "And, you might get a silver coin in return, if you do a good job!"

"Wow! Thanks, Frank! Thanks, Buster!" cried Mitzi, and she rushed off into town. She was in *such* a hurry that she forgot to take the silver coin from Ned for cleaning his windows!

First Mitzi went to Sammy's shop, where she worked very hard indeed. She stacked shelves, sorted out the tins and swept the whole shop until it sparkled. And she kept a careful eye on her beloved carousel!

"That's a job well done, Mitzi," Sammy said and gave her a silver coin. "You've earned it!"

Then Mitzi helped George deliver his parcels. "Good job, Mitzi!" he beamed, and he gave her a silver coin too.

Finally, Mitzi helped Alice clean her scooter. It was a very messy job — but it earned her *another* shiny silver coin!

Back at the homestead, Buster's chocolate cake had nearly finished baking when Mitzi rushed inside. She grabbed her piggy bank and emptied it onto the table. Then she carefully counted all her coins.

"So, have you got enough for the carousel?" asked Frank.

"Seven, eight, nine . . . " Suddenly Mitzi wailed with despair. "I can't believe it! After all that hard work, I still haven't got enough money! How am I ever going to buy my beautiful carousel?"

Buster's cake was ready now, and he placed it down in front of her. "Maybe a piece of chocolate cake will make you feel better," said Buster kindly.

Seeing the big chocolate cake set
Frank thinking. "Hey, Buster! Maybe
Mitzi could sell slices of cake in town!"

Mitzi was confused. "But I haven't got a cake to sell!"

"Oh yes you have," smiled Buster. "You can have this one!"

So Mitzi set up a stall in town. Everybody wanted to buy a slice of the delicious chocolate cake!

Before long, Mitzi's moneybox was full up to the top. The moment had come to count the coins! With trembling fingers, Mitzi added them all together.

"Fourteen!" she moaned. "I'm still one short! What am I going to do?"

Then, suddenly, Ned pulled a shiny silver coin from his pocket. "Will this one help, Mitzi?" he asked. "It's for cleaning my windows."

"Oh, wow!" yelled Mitzi. "Thanks, Ned! Thanks a lot!" She grabbed him and gave him a huge hug.

Mitzi carefully carried her fifteen shiny silver coins over to Sammy's shop. Frank, Buster, Ned and the others waited outside for her.

Mitzi burst out of Sammy's shop, clutching the carousel. She was so happy, she couldn't even speak!

Frank and Buster smiled at each other. They were there to help — and this was another job well done.

Mitzi had worked very hard to get
the carousel. But she found that
the best thing about having such
a wonderful toy was being able
to share it with all her friends.